CLASSIC
StoryTellers

F. SCOTT FITZGERALD

Newport Public Library

Mitchell Lane
PUBLISHERS

P.O. Box 196
Hockessin, Delaware 19707

Titles in the Series

Judy Blume

Stephen Crane

F. Scott Fitzgerald

Ernest Hemingway

Jack London

Katherine Paterson

Edgar Allan Poe

John Steinbeck

Harriett Beecher Stowe

Mildred Taylor

Mark Twain

E.B. White

C L A S S I C
StoryTellers

F. SCOTT FITZGERALD

by John Bankston

Mitchell Lane
PUBLISHERS

Printing   1   2   3   4   5   6   7   8
     Library of Congress Cataloging-in-Publication Data

Bankston, John, 1974-
     F. Scott Fitzgerald / John Bankston.
              p. cm. — (Classic Storytellers)
     Includes bibliographical references (p.) and index.
     Contents: The struggle — Writing from memories — The most beautiful girl in the world — City of forgotten nights — The crack-up.
     ISBN 1-58415-249-4 (lib bdg.)
     1. Fitzgerald, F. Scott (Francis Scott), 1896-1940 — Juvenile literature. 2. Authors, American — 20th century — Biography — Juvenile literature. [1. Fitzgerald, F. Scott (Francis Scott), 1896-1940. 2. Authors, American. 3. Authorship] I. Title. II. Series.
     PS3511.I9Z55768 2004
     813'.52 — dc22

                                                            2003024124

ABOUT THE AUTHOR: Born in Boston, Massachusetts, John Bankston has written over three dozen biographies for young adults profiling scientists like Jonas Salk and Alexander Fleming, celebrities like Mandy Moore and Alicia Keys, great achievers like Alfred Nobel, and master musicians like Mozart. He worked in Los Angeles, California as a producer, screenwriter and actor. Currrently he is in preproduction on *Dancing at the Edge*, a semi-autobiographical film he hopes to film in Portland, Oregon. Last year he completed his first young adult novel, *18 to Look Younger.*

PHOTO CREDITS: Cover: Corbis; pp.1, 3, 6 Corbis; p. 10 Getty Images; p. 20 Hulton Archive; p. 30 Getty Images; p. 36 Hulton Archive; p. 38 Getty Images

PUBLISHER'S NOTE: This story is based on the author's extensive research, which he believes to be accurate. Documentation of such research is contained on page 46.

The internet sites referenced herein were active as of the publication date. Due to the fleeting nature of some web sites, we cannot guarantee they will all be active when you are reading this book.

Contents

F. SCOTT FITZGERALD
by John Bankston

*For Your Information

F. Scott Fitzgerald's books sell better today than they did when he was alive. To date Scribner's Publishing company has sold more than 15,000,000 copies of his books.

Chapter 1

THE STRUGGLE

Scott was sure his heart was broken. Zelda Sayre, the woman he loved, had just called off their engagement. She said he didn't make enough money to support them. She was right. It was June, 1919. At that time, a man was expected to earn a decent living before he got married. All Scott wanted was to be a successful writer with Zelda by his side. Instead, he lived in a drab and cramped apartment. He decorated its dirty walls with over 100 rejection slips from magazines that didn't want the stories he'd written. His only paycheck came from writing ad copy such as "We keep you clean in Muscatine." The client was a laundry in an Iowa town. He was miserable.

"I was a failure," he later recalled in *The Crack-Up*, "mediocre at advertising work and unable to get started as a writer. Hating the city, I got roaring, weeping drunk on my last penny and went home."[1]

Scott was 22 years old, a college dropout whose novel had been refused by the only publishing house he had a connection with. Completely broke, he was forced to move back in with his family. He was sure his life was over.

It wasn't, not by a long shot.

Scott would soon become a published novelist. Then he'd marry Zelda—for better or worse. More than 80 years later, the books he wrote are still widely read. He defined the 1920s, calling it the "Jazz Age." His work and his life reflected both the excitement of the decade and the misery of the Great Depression that followed. His life can't be separated from his art.

He was indeed a Classic Storyteller, but like many great artists he had to suffer for his work. Scott's writing came from dealing with pain: the pain and insecurity he absorbed as a little boy, the pain of his marriage to Zelda, and the pain of struggling with alcoholism.

Although many of the characters Scott described in his stories seemed well off, they usually worried about money. The challenge of living a certain lifestyle—"keeping up appearances"—was one Scott knew intimately as a writer. While many authors are talented at creating sympathy for characters who are poor, Scott could get readers rooting for characters who were rich.

During his brief lifetime, Scott sometimes earned more than $1,000 a week from writing at a time when many families earned less than that in an entire year. Yet he spent his money as fast as he made it. Because of his debts, some of which came from his wife's medical expenses, Scott was forced to write short stories for magazines just to pay the bills. Many of these stories weren't very good. Yet the four novels he completed are still read and enjoyed not just as accurate reflections of the times in which he lived, but as reflections of his life as well.

FYInfo

The Jazz Age

Louis Armstrong

In the late 1950s, most teenagers in the United States began to play rock n' roll in their bedrooms and in their cars. Inspired by blues music from the Mississippi River Delta region, the music made stars of artists like Elvis Presley and Chuck Berry. In just a few years it became background music for the rebellious youth of the 1960s. It created a sense of alienation, or separation, from the "older generation," parents who just didn't "get" the music their kids were listening to. Many of those parents had grown up listening to jazz. Thirty years before rock n' roll arrived on the scene, it had made their parents just as nervous.

Jazz has been called the only art form created in America. It sprang from the Dixieland and ragtime rhythms of New Orleans, Louisiana, and used the same kinds of improvisational styles. It was the soundtrack for the 1920s, the music of illegal bars called speakeasies, nightclubs and even movies.

Jazz originated among African-Americans (just like the Delta Blues which inspired rock n' roll) and made stars out of performers like Louis Armstrong, Bessie Smith and Fats Waller. Soon white artists like Benny Goodman and George Gershwin picked up the style as well.
Just as parents in the new millennium are distressed by the lifestyles associated with hip-hop and techno, parents in the 1920s were shocked by the behavior of the teens and 20-somethings who listened to jazz. Jazz fans seemed to smoke more and drink more. Women who liked jazz often wore skirts that were much shorter than those of "good girls."

In 1927, the Warner Brothers movie studio introduced talkies with *The Jazz Singer,* starring Al Jolson. From its immortal first spoken line, "You ain't seen nothin' yet," the film fascinated audiences and earned a then-record three million dollars at the box office.

"The Jazz Age is over,"[1] F. Scott Fitzgerald claimed in a 1931 letter to his editor, Maxwell Perkins. Fitzgerald had given the 1920s its name in *Tales of the Jazz Age,* a collection of his short stories that had been published less than 10 years earlier. He realized that with the Great Depression crippling the country, the free-spirited decade of the Roaring 20s was just a memory. But jazz, the music of the times, has endured.

9

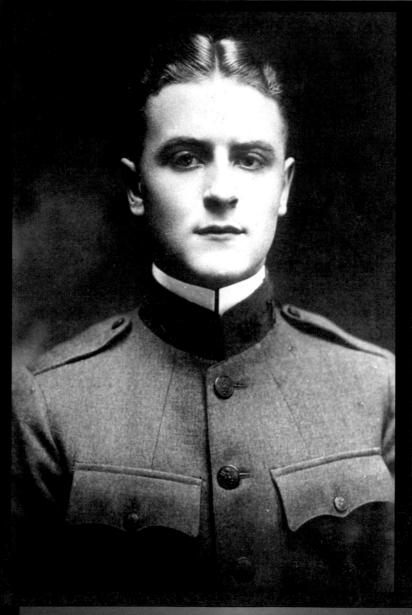

Wanting a life of adventure Scott joined the army so he could fight in World War I. Scott met Zelda Sayre when he was stationed in her home town of Montgomery, Alabama.

Chapter 2

WRITING FROM MEMORIES

No one came to Scott's seventh birthday party even though he'd given out invitations to his classmates in Buffalo, New York. Scott and his mother had carefully planned the event. They hung decorations; his mother baked a cake. As a rainstorm swept over his family's home, Scott looked at his mother and tried not to cry.

As a consolation, she let him eat the entire birthday cake by himself. Scott's unpopularity wasn't entirely his fault. Although the weather helped turn the party into a wash, Scott had only recently come to Buffalo. His family had moved several times and he wasn't very good at making friends. Usually he showed off or bragged about how good he was at sports. He made up a lot of things.

Scott felt like he was on the outside looking in. It could be lonely, but it was excellent training for a writer.

Francis Scott Key Fitzgerald was born on September 24, 1896 in St. Paul, Minnesota to Edward and Mollie Fitzgerald. He was related to Frances Scott Key, who in 1814 wrote "The Star Spangled Banner." Scott—he was never called anything else—spent his infancy in a rented apartment. His mother had lost two daughters to illness when they were one and three. She was especially careful with her newborn son.

Their apartment lay in the shadows of Summit Hill, the wealthiest neighborhood in St. Paul. It was a street lined mainly with old homes and older money—families who'd inherited their wealth. Scott worshipped men like James J. Hill, who owned the largest mansion on the hill. Hill grew up poor, yet he made millions in the railroads. Scott often imagined what life was like in the homes that overlooked his own.

The Fitzgeralds weren't poor, but they weren't rich either. They were middle class. To Scott that was the worst class of them all. His father's inability to provide for his family didn't help. Edward was born in Maryland eight years before the start of the Civil War, and often told stories about those times. Scott picked up some of his imagination from his father, but it was Mollie who influenced his aspiration to join the upper class. She'd grown up privileged in St. Paul, and toured Europe four times before her husband took her to Paris on their honeymoon. She was bored by the city, even as he rushed to take in the unfamiliar sights.

"I am half black Irish and half old American stock," Scott wrote much later in his life. "The black Irish side of my family had the money and looked down upon the Maryland side of the family who had breeding."[1]

The differences in their backgrounds contributed to the arguments between Mollie and Edward. Money was a constant worry. Life became even more challenging when Edward's furniture business failed in 1898. The family moved to Buffalo, New York. Edward went from owning a business to selling soap for a living. He barely managed to support his family, which had grown larger with the arrival of Scott's sister Annabel in 1901.

Soon they moved to Syracuse, New York, where they spent two years. Then they returned to Buffalo just before Scott's unhappy seventh birthday party. By now he was interested in reading. Soon he would begin writing. At the age of 10 he won his first awards, for essays he wrote in school. He even tried to write a detective story.

His life wasn't all about books. "Although he was a small boy, he competed for athletic recognition because sports were a way to distinction or even power among his friends,"[2] says biographer Matthew Bruccoli.

Then disaster struck. "One afternoon —I was ten or eleven — the phone rang and my mother answered it," Scott later recalled in a letter. "I didn't understand what she said, but I felt that disaster had come to us. My mother, a little while back had given me a quarter to go swimming. I gave the money back to her. I knew something terrible had happened and I thought she could not spare the money now."[3]

He was right. Edward had been fired. Whatever façade he'd constructed blew apart as the family was forced to stay briefly with Mollie's mother in St. Paul, then move to a series of other houses and apartments almost every year. It was a humiliating experience. Writing was the best escape Scott knew when he was a kid. The world he created with paper and pen kept him going through hard times. Attending a day school, St. Paul's Academy, he began playwriting for his school's theater program and penning stories for the school newspaper. His first published story, "The Mystery of the Raymond Mortgage," was written when he was 13. Inspired by Edgar Allan Poe's "The Murders in the Rue Morgue," it was the first of many stories in which Scott drew inspiration from the great writers who came before him.

The only thing Scott could focus on in school was writing stories and plays. His grades were terrible. In the end, the family decided he'd be better off in a stricter environment. With money borrowed from Mollie's mother, Scott was sent to boarding school. Most teens would be nervous about going away, homesick and not looking forward to sharing a small room with strangers. Scott was overjoyed when he arrived at The Newman School in Hackensack, New Jersey in the fall of 1911.

On the long train ride, he'd imagined entering the private world of upper class Easterners his mother taught him to admire. He was sure his classmates could offer him access to the best families, clubs and parties. The school would be a ticket to the Ivy League—prestigious colleges like Dartmouth, Harvard, Yale and Princeton.

Scott's fantasies and reality never quite caught up with each other. Again he tried to make friends by bragging about his athletic ability. He even wrote an unsigned article in the school paper describing the football talents of Scott Fitzgerald! Though he was often alone, Scott refused to give in to loneliness. He used his solitude to create more short stories. Money was still a problem at home. Ivy League colleges cost over $300 a year, ten times a state school's tuition. Besides, Scott's grades at Newman were far from Ivy League material.

When his grandmother died and left his mother $125,000, his fortunes improved. Now his mother could afford to send him to Princeton, the college of his choice with its rolling green lawns and country club atmosphere. Again Scott let his imagination run wild as he envisioned a life of educational leisure, filled with deep conversations about life and art with boys (back then Princeton didn't admit girls) from the best families.

But that didn't change his grades. In order to have a shot at attending, Scott needed to do well on the admissions test. Although his scores in English were outstanding, the rest weren't—fairly surprising considering rumors that he may have cheated. At first he was refused admission. He appeared at the school in person and persuaded the admissions committee to change its mind. There was one condition. He would have to pass exams in algebra, physics, Latin and French by December or be kicked out. Besides studying for those tests, he also had to take French literature, Roman history, trigonometry and English composition. It was an incredibly tough course load for even a disciplined student. For Scott it was impossible.

Scott still made time to try out for the football team, pretty ambitious for someone who stood just five feet, eight inches tall and weighed only 140 pounds. He was cut the first day.

Unable to play football, his course load keeping him from other extra-curricular activities, Scott still made time for writing. A lot of writing. During his time at Princeton, two dozen of Scott's stories were published in the school's literary magazine, *The Nassau Literary Magazine*, and another three dozen in its humor magazine, the *Tiger*. He also wrote the lyrics for three musicals.

Unfortunately, Scott didn't put nearly as much effort into his schoolwork. Although he barely passed his exams in December his grades were horrible. He hated trigonometry, hated Latin and even hated English, where he complained the entire department was "top heavy and undistinguished with an uncanny knack for making literature distasteful to young men."[4]

Although he desperately wanted to be a professional writer, Scott wasn't well read. He got into arguments over books he'd only glanced at in libraries. His education at Princeton didn't take place in the classroom, but in dorm rooms, in nearby bars and at the Cottage, an eating club he joined during his sophomore year.

Two classmates in particular influenced Scott's reading and later his writing. Both John Pearle Bishop and Edmund Wilson came from established, East Coast families and they'd received top-notch prep schooling. They were more amused than irritated by Scott's tendency to discuss books he hadn't read. The two became important and influential friends.

He would need them. Scott's grades kept him from experiencing the Princeton of his dreams. The Triangle Club put on a musical every Christmas which toured to a dozen cities. For three years Scott wrote the musicals, but his sub-par grades kept him off the stage.

His disappointment was tempered when he was allowed to travel with the group and appear in newspaper advertisements promoting the show. Like the plays in William Shakespeare's time, all of the parts—both male and female—were played by men. In the ad, Scott dressed in a blonde wig, make-up and gown. His friends joked that he made a pretty girl. He must have. When he attended a party at the University of Minnesota in full drag, his ruse wasn't discovered until he had to use the bathroom.

In 1915, Scott contracted malaria and left school. It was a good excuse to leave because he was in danger of being expelled. He returned in the fall of 1916 to repeat his junior year. By then his mind was elsewhere. He was sick of school, sick of studying, sick of his cramped and dreary dorm room. He wanted to be a professional writer. He wanted adventure.

The adventure he dreamed of was taking place thousands of miles away across the Atlantic Ocean. The Great War (later called World War I) began with the assassination of Austrian Archduke Franz Ferdinand in 1914 and ended more than four years later with the deaths of millions across Europe. By the spring of 1917, the German invasion of France had been at a bloody standstill for two and a half years. The two armies faced off in trenches only a hundred years apart. The space between them was called "No Man's Land" with good reason. Machine guns ripped apart thousands of men on both sides as they tried to break the stalemate. It was a brutal conflict, the first big war of the 20th century. Modern weapons combined with old-fashioned tactics to produce stunning numbers of casualties. Even though President Woodrow Wilson committed United States forces in April, 1917, it was opposed by many Americans who wanted to stay out of the war.

Scott wasn't one of them. He wanted a romantic adventure he could write stories about. Although he'd never experienced anything worse than a fistfight, he saw himself as an officer, valiantly leading his men into combat. "I may get killed for America, but I'm going to die for myself,"[5] he wrote in a letter to his cousin Cecilia Taylor.

Scott dropped out of school. In November, 1917, he arrived at Fort Leavenworth, Kansas for officer training. The man in charge of his platoon was Dwight D. Eisenhower, the future U.S. President 35 years later. Scott would become an infantry lieutenant, a very dangerous job. He was well aware of the danger. He wanted to leave behind a novel in the likely event of his being killed. During the time he was supposed to be studying military tactics he scribbled the outline for what he entitled *The Romantic Egotist*. After that ruse was discovered, Scott spent his weekends in the officers' club, writing with dedication at a small table amidst the smoke, noise and drinking. By the time his training was finished in February, so was his novel.

To increase his chances of having the novel published, Scott used his Princeton connections. Several members of the Charles Scribner's Sons publishing company had attended the school. Even better, one of Scott's friends was Shane Leslie, an author whose books were published by Scribner's. Leslie made a few minor corrections to Scott's manuscript and sent it to editor Maxwell Perkins.

The Romantic Egotist was raw and uncontrolled. It was more like a collection of well-written scenes than an actual novel. It described Princeton life from a former student's perspective. The world Scott wrote about was unfamiliar to older people. It was also one of the first books to depict "flappers," women who smoked, and drank and partied just as much as the men. Perkins was sure he had something extraordinary on his hands. Scott spoke with an authentic voice. It was as if a member of his generation was clearly speaking through the novel's words.

Beyond its style, the book's main chance for decent sales was the author's potential mortality. Most infantry lieutenants didn't survive very long. A young English army officer and poet named Rupert Brooke died en route to battle a year after the beginning of the war. Sales of his works quickly increased.

Despite all that *The Romantic Egotist* had going for it, in the end the publisher rejected it. Scott received a long personal letter from Perkins in August, 1918, encouraging him to carefully revise the book and send it back. It wasn't good news, but it wasn't exactly bad news either. By that time, Scott had more on his mind than getting his book published.

FYInfo

The Flappers

"I am assuming that the Flapper will live by her accomplishments and not by her Flapping,"[1] Zelda Fitzgerald wrote in 1922 in a humorous magazine article entitled "Eulogy on the Flapper." To some people, the idea of a "flapper" accomplishing anything was ridiculous.

Clara Bow

The term originated soon after the end of World War I. It referred to young women who began acting in non-traditional ways. Some historians believe that the term "flapper" came from the image of young birds flapping their wings as they tried to fly.

In many ways the mere existence and popularity of flappers was a sign of accomplishment. Flappers celebrated women's new-found freedom in the 1920s, freedom which began when they earned the right to vote in 1920 with the passage of the Nineteenth Amendment. Social freedom quickly followed as barriers eroded. In some ways the freedom also came because alcohol was illegal. Anyone who was willing to go to a speakeasy to drink was probably not expected to behave herself.

Like many young women today, flappers took their fashion cues from movie stars. Silent screen legend Clara Bow wore her hair short in a bob, and millions of women imitated her. They wore dresses that hung loosely, and gave up corsets. Without that device holding them in, women began to worry about their weight. Their hemlines began to rise, reaching even above the knee. This showed off their silk stockings and garter belts, so casually revealed during the frantic moves of popular dances such as the Charleston and the shimmy. Flappers smoked and drank and kissed men in public and wore heavy makeup. They didn't just ride in automobiles, they also drove them. They wanted to work *and* they wanted to get married. They were in many ways the first generation of American women striving for equality. Perhaps Zelda was right. The Flappers did more than just "Flapping."

Although Zelda had many eligible suitors, it was Scott who won her heart and hand in marriage. While Zelda's father disapproved of Scott, her mother admired the young writer.

Chapter 3

THE MOST BEAUTIFUL GIRL IN THE WORLD

Zelda Sayre was the type of girl who was so beautiful that other girls would leave a party if she showed up. At the age of 18, she'd perfected the skill of holding a man's attention. Her petite figure, blonde hair (which she wore loose, in opposition to the standards of the time) and perfect complexion did most of the work. She was the daughter of an Alabama Supreme Court justice, but in her hometown of Montgomery she had a reputation for trouble.

Born with the new century in 1900, by 1918 Zelda smoked a lot, drank more than she smoked, and dated more than she drank. She was a modern girl in a period when women still didn't have the right to vote. She didn't care what people thought of her.

Her mother and father, Minnie and Anthony, were respected and socially prominent. They were not rich, but Zelda came from the type of casually sophisticated background Scott admired. They met at a country club dance when he was stationed in Montgomery, waiting to be shipped out to a war he didn't think he'd survive. In the dress uniform of an officer, the slim 22-year-old looked dashing. In reality he was a college dropout with a rejected novel and few prospects. As Zelda's family may have noted, F. Scott Fitzgerald was not marriage material. Even if he had been, he was half Irish—a mark against him in the Anglo-Saxon South. Just as bad, he seemed to have a drinking problem.

"But he's so nice when he's sober,"[1] Zelda is supposed to have said to her father.

"He's never sober,"[2] the judge replied.

The judge may have been right, but the two had chemistry. Despite the difference in their backgrounds, they were actually quite similar. They were both spoiled and immature, used to getting their way and being the center of attention. They both had a hard time understanding another person's point of view. They even looked so much alike that some thought they were brother and sister.

It was love at first sight.

"I've always known that any girl who gets stewed in public, who frankly enjoys and tells shocking stories, who smokes casually and makes the remark that she has 'kissed thousands of men and intends to kiss thousands more,' cannot be considered beyond reproach or even above it," Scott was quoted in a biography of Zelda. "I fell in love with her courage, her sincerity and her flaming self respect. I love her and that's the beginning and end of everything."[3]

Scott may not have had any prospects, while Zelda was overflowing with them. The most eligible men in the South pursued her from the time she was old enough to date. She accumulated plenty of marriage proposals. Scott's was just one of many in a long string. Yet it was Scott who won Zelda's heart and her attention. Maybe it was his unsuitability that made him so attractive, a good way to get back at her conservative, prejudiced father. Or maybe, like the Scribner's publishing house, she expected him to meet a tragic end.

That tragic end would have to wait. The Great War concluded with an armistice in November, 1918 just before Scott was due to be sent overseas. After a few disastrous military jobs, Scott was discharged the following February. By then he and Zelda were engaged. Scott moved to New York City and struggled to find writing work. He settled for a bad job with a mediocre ad agency, where his pay was just 35 dollars a week. Zelda knew she could never survive on so little money. She taunted him with stories about kissing other men and her long list of wealthy suitors.

By June, Zelda had enough of Scott and his struggles. She broke off the engagement. Scott quit his job and spent his last dollar on a train ticket home and a bottle of gin.

In the summer of 1919 he arrived at the family house, now situated on upscale Summit Hill. The improvement in his family's location did nothing to ease his sense of failure. With nothing to lose, Scott labored on the revisions to *The Romantic Egotist*. All he had was hope and the encouraging letter from Maxwell Perkins.

At least there were no distractions. Alone and unemployed, Scott worked harder on the book than he'd ever worked before. He tightened the material by eliminating parts that didn't flow, improved the story, and developed the characters. Other than a new friendship with future author Donald Ogden Stewart, Scott had a limited social life. The focus helped.

By early September he was done. He sent the revised manuscript (now re-titled *This Side of Paradise*) to Maxwell Perkins at Scribner's. He hoped the news would be better this time. He didn't have long to wait.

Within two weeks, Perkins sent him a letter praising the work he'd done and congratulating him. Scribner's would publish the book.

"I'd taken a job repairing car roofs at the Northern Pacific Shops," Scott recalled in *The Crack-Up*. "Then the postman rang and that day I quit work and ran along the streets, stopping automobiles to tell friends and acquaintances about it—my novel *This Side of Paradise* was accepted for publication. I paid off my small debts, bought a suit and woke up every morning with a world of ineffable [indescribable] top loftiness and promise."[4]

He returned to New York. The work he'd done on *This Side of Paradise* was a better education than the one he'd gotten at Princeton. The still unknown novelist got an agent, Harold Ober, who began selling stories to the same magazines that had rejected him only a few months earlier. His stories appeared in *The Smart Set* and *The Saturday Evening Post*, which had a circulation of three million. The magazine would eventually pay Scott $4,000 a story.

Flush with the confidence of newfound success, Scott briefly dated an English actress named Rosalind Fuller. The relationship was a poor substitute for Zelda. Scott still loved her.

As winter's chill crept into the city, Scott retreated south to a New Orleans boarding house to write. While there he traveled to Montgomery and persuaded Zelda to give him another chance. The two soon were re-engaged. She would later admit that his potential fame was a deciding factor.

Although Zelda's father could only offer a reluctant blessing (he still saw Scott as an unreliable drunk) her mother admired the young writer. She warned him about the challenges he'd face with her daughter. Scott didn't realize how accurate Mrs. Sayre was.

Zelda and Scott were married on April 3, 1920 in New York's St. Patrick's Cathedral. None of their parents attended. It was another untraditional touch for a thoroughly untraditional couple who briefly lived together before the ceremony.

This Side of Paradise had been released the week before. Its first printing of 3,000 copies sold out in three days. Before 1921 was over it would go through a dozen printings and sell more than 50,000 copies. In the 1920s, this type of best-seller for a first time, unknown novelist was unprecedented. Scott's talent was one reason for the book's popularity, along with numerous praising reviews, but that was only part of it. Success in publishing, like most things, is a matter of timing. Scott's timing could not have been better. He wrote a college novel at a time when many more young people were going to college. He was the voice of a young generation when youth culture was first being celebrated in silent films and magazines. After the horrors of war, the country was ready for a giant party. The Fitzgeralds were on the guest list.

In many ways, the decade was influenced by two amendments to the Constitution. Both became law in 1920. The Nineteenth Amendment increased freedom, giving women the right to vote for the first time. Many believed this was just an initial step toward an equal society. The Eighteenth Amendment, however, restricted freedom—the freedom to drink. The amendment was more commonly called Prohibition. It forbade the sale or manufacture of alcohol. It was still legal to drink in a private home.

To evade the law, many bars converted to speakeasies. These were hidden clubs that required a secret knock or a password for admission. To keep from getting shut down, speakeasy owners bribed police and elected officials. As a result, crime and corruption increased greatly in the 1920s. That was one of the reasons why the amendment would be repealed in 1933.

Drinking at speakeasies and other illegal establishments became a way of life for the Fitzgeralds. At the time his novel became a best-seller, Scott was 23 and his wife was 19. They were photographed nearly as often as the stars of the silent screen. They loved the attention.

Scott suddenly had money. He quickly got to work spending it. The boy who'd roomed with richer boys in boarding school and college set about to style himself in their image. He and Zelda bought the best clothes, stayed in five-star hotels and traveled first class by train and ship. When they weren't shopping they were drinking.

Scott saw getting drunk as a way of gaining experiences, and dealing with whatever he couldn't deal with sober. For Zelda it was the fastest cure she knew for boredom. Alcohol wasn't the answer but Scott had forgotten the question—he was the kind of alcoholic who was out of control with only a few drinks. When he drank he was volatile, he started arguments and got into fights. He and Zelda argued constantly, although she said his pain increased her passion.

As bad as the drinking was on Scott's body, it was worse on his mind. He had a hard time focusing on a novel, and even if he could there were bills to pay. At a time when many families lived on $1,000 a year, Scott earned over thirty times that much writing short stories.

Spending money and going to jazz clubs and speakeasies, the couple became a living embodiment of the 1920s.

A year after their marriage, Zelda learned she was pregnant. The couple decided to take a trip to Europe before she was too far along to travel. They toured Italy, England and France, sowing the initial seeds for living abroad. During the next 10 years

The Eiffel Tower in Paris, France was built in 1889 to commemorate the 100 year anniversiary of the French Revolution. Pictured here today, the Eiffel Tower looks the same as it did when Scott and Zelda lived in Paris.

they would spend half their time in Europe, joining many other Americans who had left the United States for the freer lifestyles of Europe.

On October 26, 1921, Frances Scott Fitzgerald was born in St. Paul. Her parents would call her "Scottie." After giving birth Zelda said, "I hope it's beautiful and a fool—a beautiful little fool."⁵ Like many of Zelda's remarks, it eventually found its way into one of Scott's books.

Scott's second novel, *The Beautiful and Damned*, was released the following year. Praised by critics and snapped up by readers, it sold even better than *This Side of Paradise*. Scott began to truly believe he could have a brilliant career as a novelist, and that soon he wouldn't have to write stories for magazines at all. In *The Beautiful and Damned*, the hero Anthony Patch spends much of the book spending money he doesn't have until he is rescued by fortune. Scott could only hope that his fortune was right around the corner.

FYInfo

A Moveable Feast

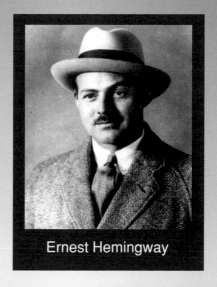

Ernest Hemingway

By 1925, thousands of Americans were living in Paris. Sometimes it seemed as if all of them were busy writing or painting, or dating writers and painters. The Americans—called expatriates—were drawn to a city without Prohibition, the U.S. law banning the sale or manufacture of alcohol. Many types of behavior that would land someone in jail back in the United States were ignored in Paris. It was the ideal environment for a wild couple like Zelda and Scott Fitzgerald.

They made the most of it, partying in the city's nightlife and taking in its café culture, casual outdoor spots where creative types gathered. Still, in many ways, the Fitzgeralds were isolated from the city's more bohemian, outsider arts community. By staying in expensive hotels and living in apartments in the best neighborhoods, the Fitzgeralds had very little contact with struggling artists. Most of their acquaintances were established and successful, like James Joyce and Gertrude Stein (who coined the phrase "Lost Generation" to describe the post-war wanderers such as Scott and Zelda).

The one struggling artist Scott befriended was Ernest Hemingway. He came to Paris in 1921 and spent several years surviving on his wife's money while trying to write for a living. But he would be as well known and well paid as Fitzgerald with the publication in 1926 of his first novel, *The Sun Also Rises*. It owed part of its success to the environment of Paris, which nurtured developing talents in a way that few other cities could have. Even though he was so poor that sometimes he had to eat pigeons, he felt that Paris was very rich in experiences that he could use in his writing. Hemingway would later describe his experiences as an expatriate in Paris in the book *A Moveable Feast.*

For Scott it was Zelda. He was willing to ignore whatever bad traits she had.

After a short stay in Paris, the Fitzgeralds relocated to the French Riviera on the Mediterranean Sea. They befriended Gerald and Sara Murphy, a wealthy couple with a taste for artistic types. They tolerated Zelda and Scott's excesses and would later be fictionalized by Scott in several stories.

On the Riviera, Scott would not allow himself to be distracted by Zelda's demands. He focused on his next novel, *The Great Gatsby*. She was bored and sought her own diversions. In the summer of 1924 she became involved with Edouard Jozan, a French pilot. It was probably not much more serious than the flirtations that Zelda had enjoyed as a popular teenager in Mississippi. That didn't matter to Scott. He was devastated. "That September 1924, I knew something had happened that could never be replaced,"[1] he said years later.

Some people say that all novelists have one great novel in them. For Scott that novel was *The Great Gatsby*. It tells the story of upstart, born-poor Jimmy Gatz. He transforms himself into a wealthy self-made man named Jay Gatsby. The source of his wealth is mysterious, and quite likely is illegal. Years earlier, the woman he loves had turned him down and married a rich man. Gatsby hopes that by becoming rich he can win her back. Although Scott had finished the book by the fall of 1924, he revised it until the very end. He even labored over the galleys. Those are pages that writers receive just before a book is scheduled to be published. They are typeset, the words are in place. Authors are only expected to double-check for errors. Instead, Scott often changed entire sections, forcing the book to be typeset again. He continued to make revisions until the last possible moment.

Critically, all the changes were worth the effort that Scott put in. Most reviewers believed that Scott had fulfilled the promise of his early career. Today *The Great Gatsby* is considered a classic.

In 1925, it was a disappointment. The same readers who stood in line to buy *This Side of Paradise* and *The Beautiful and Damned* almost ignored *Gatsby*. The novel sold fewer than 24,000 copies when it was released; Scott made less than $7,000 in royalties.

However, when the Fitzgeralds moved back to Paris in April, 1925, Scott didn't realize how little money his book was going to make. At that moment he was a successful writer still in his 20s, accompanied by his stylish wife and beautiful young daughter, Scottie. He felt as if he had the world at his command.

Soon he met a struggling young writer named Ernest Hemingway. They quickly formed a strong, if competitive, friendship. The pair could not have been more different. Ernest had fought in the war Scott couldn't get into, he was tough and rugged, over six feet tall and a muscular 180 pounds. Although he thought Scott was too sensitive and couldn't handle his liquor, he admired the slightly older man's talent and success.

"Scott was a man who looked like a boy with a face between handsome and pretty," Hemingway recalled in *The Moveable Feast*. "The mouth worried you until you knew him and then it worried you more."[2]

Zelda and Ernest hated each other on sight. She didn't believe anyone could be as macho as Ernest unless he was hiding something. He thought Zelda was crazy and kept Scott from working. In a way, they were both right. Scott did everything he could for Ernest, sending his early writings to Maxwell Perkins. Scribner's would soon begin publishing Ernest's novels.

Chapter 4 CITY OF FORGOTTEN NIGHTS

It didn't take long for Zelda to become notorious for taking off her clothes in public places. She was also jealous of Scott. When he met the famous dancer Isadora Duncan at a restaurant, Scott was his usually silly self, kneeling at her feet and letting the older woman run her fingers through his hair. Zelda was enraged. She rose from their table, and threw herself down a flight of stairs. Her injuries were minor but she got Scott's attention.

By the time Christmas rolled around, the Fitzgeralds were ready to return to America. They boarded a ship bound for the United States. They traveled to Washington, D.C., where Scott's parents now lived, and then to Montgomery to see Zelda's folks. During their vacation, Scott received an offer he couldn't refuse. A Hollywood producer wanted him to write a movie. Scott was broke. He couldn't turn down the job.

FYInfo

Famous Writers and Hollywood

Scott Fitzgerald's flirtation with Hollywood was not the first time that a novelist became involved with Tinseltown. In the 1920s and 1930s, well-known authors like Thomas Mann, Bertolt Brecht and William Faulkner all labored at one time or another for motion picture studios. The reason was simple: money.

No matter how well a novel sold, Hollywood producers were always able to pay a writer more than he could make on book sales. After all, far more people went to the movies than bought books. In 1932, Faulkner made $6,000 when he sold one of his stories to Hollywood. A few years later, Scott would make over $1,000 a week in the studios.

When movies began, they were silent. In many cases, comic actors from vaudeville were hired as scenarists. Their job was to think up comic incidents that could be filmed. It wasn't until sound and "talkies" that writers had to be hired to write dialogue as well as create scenes.

In the 1930s, Scott like many other writers, was primarily employed by one studio. He often put in 10 hours a day in an office and turned out script after script. Writers were usually paid by the week, not by the screenplay. Even though their pay

was good, they had little status. Hollywood was churning out hundreds of movies every year. It was almost like working in a factory.

Today most screenwriters "freelance." That means that they aren't employed by one studio. Instead they "shop" their scripts from producer to producer. Their work is considered to be important. The situation is also different for many successful novelists of our time, such as Stephen King, J. K. Rowling, and John Grisham. They receive millions of dollars from studios that want to turn their best-selling books into movies. Once the studio has purchased the rights to make a movie, it hires one or more screenwriters to write the script.

A light-hearted family portrait of Scott dancing with Zelda and daughter Frances in front of their Christmas tree. Frances would be the only child Scott and Zelda would have.

Chapter 5

THE CRACK-UP

Scott was certain he could conquer Hollywood. Some of his stories had already been made into movies and he'd contributed dialogue to others. His conceit was no different than that of many other novelists. They were certain that books were better than movies and movies should be easier to write.

They aren't. Novels can be any shape or size, they can take place in a character's mind or span a thousand years over a thousand pages. Movies rarely last longer than two hours. At the rate of page a minute of screen time, scripts are usually no more than 120 pages. Screenplays are similar to stage plays. Maybe Scott should have learned his lesson with *The Vegetable*. It was a play he'd written in 1922. It closed in less than two months.

Scott wasn't worried. He was sure he could do it. Leaving Scottie with relatives, he and Zelda moved into a bungalow at the luxurious Ambassador

Hotel. The couple brought their usual bad behavior with them to the West Coast. They barked like dogs when they weren't on the guest list at a producer's private party, "cooked" guests' jewelry in tomato soup, and sang drunken songs at quiet dinners. In Hollywood, only movie stars could get away with such outrageous behavior. The Fitzgeralds weren't nearly as famous and loved as they'd once been. In addition, they were a bit old to behave like children.

With so many distractions, it's not surprising that Scott had trouble concentrating on his script. He soon discovered that it wasn't quite as easy to write a screenplay as he had thought it would be. Perhaps because his writing was going poorly, or maybe just to get back at Zelda, Scott became interested in another woman. She was Lois Moran, an 18-year-old Irish actress with blonde hair and blue eyes who spoke fluent French. While Scott and Lois never really had a romance, Zelda became very jealous of them. Soon afterward, Scott learned that his script had been rejected. That meant that he could only collect his $3,500 advance, rather than the full $16,000 that he'd have received if the script had been satisfactory. He and Zelda left Hollywood having spent more than the advance he'd been given.

As usual, Scott would use the experience as material for his next novel, *Tender is the Night*. Lois would become Rosemary, the 17-year-old starlet in love with the book's main character, Dick Diver. However, much of the book's inspiration came from another part of Scott's life: Zelda's mental illness.

Zelda's behavior had always been unusual. It became increasingly odd as she neared thirty and the family moved back to Europe. She began to see and hear things, she had wild mood swings, and sometimes she tried to drive off cliffs or into other cars.

She tried to put her energy into creative efforts. She painted and she wrote a novel, *Save Me the Waltz*, and several short stories. She decided to become a star ballerina, a pretty ambitious goal for a woman her age. Despite the obstacles, she was able to study with Lubov Egorova, a top Parisian instructor who felt Zelda could dance professionally.

It was not to be.

In April, 1930, Zelda suffered the first of several nervous breakdowns. She was eventually diagnosed as schizophrenic, a serious mental disorder. When she was at her sickest she had no sense of reality. Unfortunately, treatments in the 1930s weren't very effective.

Although she would be released several times, Zelda would spend much of the rest of her life in mental institutions. One result was that she and Scott didn't live together after 1934. She would die in a fire at the Highland Hospital in Asheville, North Carolina fourteen years later.

During the time that Zelda was hospitalized, Scott struggled to pay her enormous medical bills. Unfortunately the Great Depression, which began with the stock market crash in 1929, left 25 percent of working Americans without jobs. Magazine sales plummeted and so did Scott's fees. In 1932 he earned less than half of what he'd made the year before. The publication of *Tender is the Night* two years later didn't help things financially. It sold only 13,000 copies. Scott wound up owing his publisher more in advances than the book made.

By 1937, Scott was heavily in debt. Once again he turned to Hollywood. This time he managed to keep working for MGM for over a year and a half. Although he only got credit for one film, *Three Comrades*, he did a week of work on *Gone With the Wind* and sometimes managed to earn over $1,000 a week.

Chapter 5   *THE CRACK-UP*

"Seriously, I expect to dip in and out of the pictures for the rest of my natural life," he wrote Scottie, "but it is not very soul-satisfying because it is a business of telling stories fit for children."[1]

Scott was 44 years old and writing his fifth novel *The Last Tycoon* when he died. This photograph was taken four years before his fatal heartattack.

After his contract for MGM expired, Scott worked as a freelance screenwriter for the rest of his natural life. It didn't last very long. On December 21, 1940 he suffered a fatal heart attack. He was working on what would have been his fifth novel. Called *The Last Tycoon*, it is set in Hollywood and draws on his experiences there. Even though it was never finished, Scribner's published it in 1941.

Newspapers gave prominent mention to his death. The tone of the articles was expressed in the *New York Times*, which commented, "The promise of his brilliant career was never fulfilled."[2]

Time has given Scott back his reputation. His books sell better today than they ever did while he was alive. *The Great Gatsby* is often taught in high school and college. Students and the general public buy more than 300,000 copies every year. In all, Scribner's has sold more than 15,000,000 copies of his books.

As biographer Matthew Broccoli concludes, "F. Scott Fitzgerald is now permanently placed with the greatest writers who ever lived, where he wanted to be all along. Where he belongs."[3]

FYInfo

Mental Health May Make You Mad

Located near Geneva, Switzerland, the Les Rives des Prangins is a mental health clinic. Zelda Fitzgerald was admitted there in 1930 and stayed for more than a year. It could have been a country club with beautifully landscaped lawns, a tennis court and even private villas. It also had a huge price tag—more than $1,000 a month. Very few mentally ill people could afford such luxury.

"Mental hygiene" was the buzzword of the times. It reflected the belief that removing the barriers to natural capabilities was more important than actual cures. Psychiatrists focused on family backgrounds and social lives.

Zelda's diagnosis of schizophrenia was common. More than 22 percent of first time admissions to mental hospitals had such a diagnosis. The disease was believed to be a reaction of an "inadequate personality" to his or her environment.

To cure schizophrenia, doctors employed two forms of shock therapy. One was insulin shock, in which a shot of insulin sent the patient into a temporary coma.

Geneva, Switzerland

Electro convulsive therapy was more dramatic, as it required the application of electricity to the brain. It induced a seizure similar to epilepsy. Both techniques were designed to unsettle the brain patterns of the mentally ill and allow "healthy" brain patterns to take over.

In Zelda's case, therapy proved to be ineffective. She was in and out of mental institutions for the rest of her life. But she was far from being alone. By 1936 there were more than 500,000 people in mental institutions in the United States. That represented a ten-fold increase since 1870.

A shift from state mental institutions to community-based centers began during the 1960s. People who supported this shift believed that it would be easier to make patients lead more normal lives than being shut away for long periods of time.

CHRONOLOGY

1896	Born on September 24 in St. Paul, Minnesota
1898	Moves to Buffalo, New York
1908	Moves back to St. Paul
1911	Enters Newman School
1913	Enters Princeton University
1915	Drops out of Princeton
1916	Returns to Princeton
1917	Withdraws from school and becomes a second lieutenant in the Army
1918	Submits his first novel to Charles Scribner's Sons publishing company; meets Zelda Sayre
1919	Leaves Army; becomes engaged to Zelda; takes ad agency job; Zelda breaks engagement; Scribner's agrees to publish his first novel
1920	Publishes *This Side of Paradise*; marries Zelda
1921	Daughter Frances Scott Fitzgerald, nicknamed Scottie, is born on October 26
1922	Publishes *The Beautiful and Damned*
1924	Travels to France with family
1925	Publishes *The Great Gatsby*
1926	Returns to the United Sates
1927	Accepts job in Hollywood
1928	Returns to France
1930	Zelda enters mental institution for the first time
1931	Returns to the United States
1934	Publishes *Tender is the Night*
1938	*Three Comrades*, his only screenplay credit, premieres
1940	Dies from a heart attack on December 21
1948	Zelda dies in a fire
1986	Daughter Frances, noted writer for the *Washington Post* and *New York Times,* dies
1996	Literary conferences in the United States and Europe commemorate the 100th anniversary of F. Scott Fitzgerald's birth
2003	*Beautiful and Damned*, a musical based on the lives of Zelda and Scott Fitzgerald, opens in London
2004	The 7th International F. Scott Fitzgerald Conference is held in Switzerland

TIMELINE

1842 Irish Nationalist Movement, Young Ireland publishes The Nation newspaper encouraging the study of Irish history

1848 In Ireland, a revolt against the British is violently put down.

1861 The U.S. Civil War begins.

1865 The Civil War ends.

1880 French scientist Charles Lavern discovers a parasite in blood that causes malaria.

1883 New Zealand becomes the first country to give women the right to vote.

1896 The first modern Olympic Games are held in Athens, Greece.

1898 Author Ernest Hemingway is born.

1900 Stephen Crane, the author of *The Red Badge of Courage*, dies of tuberculosis at the age of 28.

1907 Sir Robert Baden-Powell founds the Boy Scouts.

1912 The *Titanic* sinks on her maiden voyage across the Atlantic Ocean; over 1500 passengers and crewmembers die.

1914 World War I begins.

1918 World War I ends.

1920 The 18th Amendment makes selling and manufacturing alcohol illegal; the 19th Amendment gives women the right to vote.

1927 The first "talkie," *The Jazz Singer*, premieres.

1929 The stock market crash precedes he Great Depression.

1933 Adolf Hitler becomes Chancellor of Germany.

1939 Film version of *Gone with the Wind* premieres; it wins a then-record eight Oscars the following year.

1940 Paintings more than 20,000 years old are discovered on the walls of a cave in Lascaux, France.

1941 The United States enters World War II.

1954 Ernest Hemingway is awarded the Nobel Prize for Literature.

1955 Actor James Dean dies in a car crash.

1961 Ernest Hemingway dies.

1963 President John F. Kennedy is assassinated.

1969 U.S. astronaut Neil Armstrong becomes the first man to walk on the moon.

1974 Robert Redford stars in film version of *The Great Gatsby*.

1981 British Prince Charles marries Diana Spencer, who becomes "Princess Di."

1988 Compact discs outsell long-playing records (LPs) for the first time.

1994 O.J. Simpson is accused of murdering his wife and a friend of hers.

1995 Astronaut Bernard Harris becomes first African-American to walk in space.

2003 J.K. Rowling publishes *Harry Potter and the Order of the Phoenix*.

2004 The summer Olympic Games are held in their birthplace of Athens, Greece.

CHAPTER NOTES

Chapter 1
The Struggle
1. F. Scott Fitzgerald and Edmund Wilson (editor), *The Crack-Up* (New York: New Directions, 1993), p. 26.
FYI: The Jazz Age
1. Andrew Turnbull (editor), *The Letters of F. Scott Fitzgerald* (New York: Scribner's, 1963), p. 249.
Chapter 2
Writing from Memories
1. Matthew J. Bruccoli (editor), *F. Scott Fitzgerald: A Life in Letters* (New York: Scribner's, 1994), p. 233.
2. Matthew J. Bruccoli, *Some Sort of Epic Grandeur: The Life of F. Scott Fitzgerald* (Columbia, South Carolina: University of South Carolina Press, 2002), p. 18.
3. Jeffrey Meyers, *Scott Fitzgerald: A Biography* (New York: HarperCollins, 1994), p. 9.
4. F. Scott Fitzgerald, *Afternoon of an Author* (New York: Scribner's, 1957), p. 75.
5. Jeffrey Meyers, *Scott Fitzgerald: A Biography* (New York: HarperCollins, 1994), p. 35.
FYI: The Flappers
1. Matthew J. Bruccoli (editor), *Zelda Fitzgerald: The Collected Writings* (New York: Scribner's, 1991), p. 391.
Chapter 3
The Most Beautiful Girl in the World
1. Jeffrey Meyers, *Scott Fitzgerald: A Biography* (New York: HarperCollins, 1994), p. 49.
2. Ibid.

3. Nancy Milford, *Zelda: A Biography* (New York: Harper and Row, 1970, p. 60.
4. F. Scott Fitzgerald and Edmund Wilson (editor), *The Crack-Up* (New York: New Directions, 1993), p. 21.
5. Matthew J. Bruccoli, *Some Sort of Epic Grandeur: The Life of F. Scott Fitzgerald* (Columbia, South Carolina: University of South Carolina Press, 2002), p. 156.
Chapter 4
City of Forgotten Nights
1. F. Scott Fitzgerald and Matthew Bruccoli (editor), *The Notebooks of F. Scott Fitzgerald* (New York: Harcourt Brace Jovanovich, 1978, p. 839.
2. Ernest Hemingway, *A Moveable Feast* (New York: Scribner's, 1996), p. 147.
Chapter 5
The Crack-Up
1. Matthew J. Bruccoli (editor), *F. Scott Fitzgerald: A Life in Letters* (New York: Scribner's, 1994), p. 384.
2. Matthew J. Bruccoli, *Some Sort of Epic Grandeur: The Life of F. Scott Fitzgerald* (Columbia, South Carolina: University of South Carolina Press, 2002), p. 4.
3. Ibid., p. 493.

FURTHER READING

For Young Adults

Bloom, Harold (ed.) and Norma Jean Lutz. *F. Scott Fitzgerald*. Broomall, Penn.: Chelsea House, 2001.

Brackett, Virginia. *F. Scott Fitzgerald: Writer of the Jazz Age*. Greensboro, N.C.: Morgan Reynolds, 2002.

Feinstein, Stephen. *The 1920s From Prohibition to Charles Lindbergh*. Berkeley Heights, New Jersey: Enslow Publishers, 2001.

Hakim, Joy. *War, Peace and All That Jazz*. New York: Oxford University Press Children's Books, 2002.

Lazo, Caroline Evenson. *F. Scott Fitzgerald: Voice of the Jazz Age*. Minneapolis, Minn.: Lerner Books, 2003.

Pietrusza, David. *The Roaring Twenties*. San Diego: Lucent Books, 1998.

Stewart, Gail. *The Importance of F. Scott Fitzgerald*. San Diego: Lucent Books, 1999.

Tessitore, John. *F. Scott Fitzgerald: The American Dreamer*. New York: Franklin Watts, 2001.

Works Consulted

Baughman, Judith and Matthew Bruccoli (editor). *Literary Masters: F. Scott Fitzgerald*. Detroit: Gale Group, 2000.

Bruccoli, Matthew J. (editor). *F. Scott Fitzgerald: A Life in Letters*. New York: Scribner's, 1994.

Bruccoli, Matthew J. and Margaret Duggan (editors). *Correspondence of F. Scott Fitzgerald*. New York: Random House, 1980.

Bruccoli, Matthew J. *Some Sort of Epic Grandeur: The Life of F. Scott Fitzgerald*. Columbia, South Carolina: University of South Carolina Press, 2002.

Bruccoli, Matthew J. (editor). *Zelda Fitzgerald: The Collected Writings*. New York: Scribner's, 1991.

Fitzgerald, F. Scott. *Afternoon of an Author*. New York: Scribner's, 1957.

Fitzgerald, F. Scott and Edmund Wilson (editor). *The Crack-Up*. New York: New Directions, 1993.

Fitzgerald, F. Scott and Matthew Bruccoli (editor). *The Notebooks of F. Scott Fitzgerald*. New York: Harcourt Brace Jovanovich, 1978.

Geller, Jeffrey and Marie Harris (editors). *Women of the Asylum: Voices from Behind the Walls, 1840-1945*. New York: Doubleday, 1994.

Hemingway, Ernest. *A Moveable Feast*. New York: Scribner's, 1996.

Lanahan, Eleanor (editor). *Zelda: An Illustrated Life*. New York: Harry N. Abrams, Inc., 1996.

Meyers, Jeffrey. *Scott Fitzgerald: A Biography*. New York: HarperCollins, 1994.

Milford, Nancy. *Zelda: A Biography*. New York: Harper and Row, 1970.

Turnbull, Andrew (editor). *The Letters of F. Scott Fitzgerald*. New York: Scribner's, 1963.

FURTHER READING

On the Internet

A Brief Life of Fitzgerald
    http://www.sc.edu/fitzgerald/biography.html
F. Scott Fitzgerald and the American Dream
    http://www.pbs.org/kteh/amstorytellers/bios.html
F. Scott & Zelda Fitzgerald, the lives and works of
    http://www.zeldafitzgerald.com/chronology/chronology.asp
F. Scott Fitzgerald
    http://www.literatureclassics.com/authors/Fitzgerald
Fitzgerald, F. Scott: 1896-1940
    http://www.educeth.ch/english/readinglist/fitzgeralds/index.html
Beautiful and Damned: A Musical Based on the lives of Zelda and F. Scott
    Fitzgerald
    http://www.beautifulmusical.com
Cinema — Screenwriting
    http://www.learner.org/exhibits/cinema/screenwriting.html

GLOSSARY

expatriate (ex-PAY-tree-uht)
person who leaves his or her home country to live permanently in a foreign country

flapper (FLAP-purr)
stylish, independent woman

macho (MAH-choe)
very strong sense of male pride

prohibition (pro-hib-ISH-uhn)
Eighteenth Amendment to the U.S. Constitution, passed in 1919, which made selling or manufacturing alcohol illegal

royalty (ROYAL-tee)
percentage of a book's price which its author receives

speakeasy (SPEEK-ee-zee)
illegal bar

talkie (TAW-kee)
a movie with sound and spoken dialogue

INDEX